Her Journey

Her Journey

Written by
Collene Martin

Illustrated by
Sorista Vaught

Christian Literature and Artwork
A BOLD TRUTH Publication

Her Journey

Copyright © 2018 Collene Martin
ISBN 13: 978-1-949993-00-4

● First Edition ●

BOLD TRUTH PUBLISHING
(Christian Literature & Artwork)
606 West 41st, Ste. 4
Sand Springs, Oklahoma 74063
www.BoldTruthPublishing.com

Available from Amazon.com and other retail outlets.
Orders by U.S. trade bookstores and wholesalers.
Email: boldtruthbooks@yahoo.com

Quantity sales special discounts are available on quantity purchases by corporations, associations, and others. For details, contact the publisher at the address above.

Illustrated by Sorista Vaught.

Formatting and overall design by Aaron Jones.

Printed in the USA.
11 18   10 9 8 7 6 5 4 3 2 1

Dedications

I dedicate this story to God and His mercy for all His children. I thank God for sending His son Jesus and the Holy Spirit who leads us into all truth. I also dedicate this to my loving parents who had confidence in me I didn't have. Thank You, Lord, for all that You are doing and leading us home to Heaven.

-- Collene Martin, Author

The illustrations in this book are dedicated to our Creator God. He is the source of our hopes and dreams and talents. May He be praised and honored by the art in this beautiful story. May each reader receive from God the blessing and encouragement needed to accomplish his or her journey to God's beautiful future.

-- Sorista Vaught, Illustrator

Foreword

This journey is my journey and your journey.

It is a steady walk to meet our goal and at long last we will enter the rest. My heart leaps within me at the thought of seeing Jesus Christ.

The struggles of life are our rough places along the road.

Hear what the Spirit of the Lord is saying to you, man or woman. Those struggles and your journey through life will end in triumph.

Though the title is "Her Journey," we are neither male nor female in Christ, but are Christians.

We are the person in the story.

To write something like this at 2:00a.m. is not a normal thing. I know without a doubt the Holy Spirit led me. I feel that each one who reads this will be comforted in their journey.

This will also minister to those who have lost loved ones in death.

We are the bride of Christ.

Her Journey

The young woman walked steadily toward her goal.

Her eyes were fixed on the light in the distance.

At the onset of her journey, there were those who murmured against her, those who whispered in amazement and disdain, those who called out to her, attempting to cause her to turn back. Like a moth to the flame, she was drawn to the light. This was not a pointless, hopeless action, but one of valor.

All around her she heard rumblings, wars and rumors of wars and great storms were breaking.

She heard crying and people fighting. She bravely advanced and would let nothing sidetrack her.

She walked with briars and brambles tugging at her dress and hair. She walked with determination in her step.

As she walked through the tangled mess of briars, she felt the pain of the scratches and gouges. It seemed as if she was unafraid. She felt a zeal about reaching her destination, that overcomes all the pain of her surroundings.

She had begun her undaunted trek within a matter of minutes and was not breathless, but regulated in her exertion of energy. The young woman was ageless, but somehow she had the wisdom of a weathered warrior, well trained in the matter of extended jaunts, in trials, and in battle. As she moved stealthily towards her mark, she glanced from side to side. Her road was rough and rocky, but she was not dismayed. Each step brought with it—new courage.

3

4

She had many things going through her mind as she faced the matter at hand. *"Why am I doing this? From where does this courage come? Why am I not afraid?"* These questions were all not discouraging, but instead just puzzling.

She was not the least dampened in her efforts to move forward. For some strange reason she was only exhilarated with a strange sense of confidence and longing for her destination.

Each step brought a new sense of peace.

Each step instilled joy. Each step manifested a new hope. Each step brought new release from the past. Such a strange young woman, acting as though she had never had a care in the world. She seemed somehow to be washed in determination.

The light drew closer and she was not dampened in spirit. She was not breathless nor was she discouraged.

The path had suddenly become more difficult with many obstacles to overcome. Sharp rocks pierced her young legs as she walked and even climbed over the great rocks, fraught with loose areas of pea-like gravels and sharp stones.

There were animals in the distance, but she was not afraid. She kept her eyes on the light and only peace compassed her. It was as if the sounds would deter her and perhaps the night sounds and darkness might stir a twinge of hidden fear.

There were owls and bats sweeping past at times, but she had no time to be afraid. Those things only caused her to be that much more set in reaching her goal. Unseen but present, her angels held back the unseen enemy that would attempt to intimidate her and bring her journey to a halt.

As she walked, she was aware of her unseen companions. There were angels all around her. She went step by step, trusting her Lord for a safe journey. Each day, each hour, each moment was for His Glory. The Lord had sent angels to watch over her.

She loved the Lord with all her heart. The most beautiful of fragrances was that of the presence of the Lord all around her as she prayed for those she loved and anticipated seeing many of those she had prayed for in the past. She was exhilarated at the thought of seeing the King of Kings and Lord of Lords. She had waited for this moment for years, for what seemed like ages.

It had been what seemed a long time, but her adventure deepened her sense of determination.

She longed to arrive at her destination. The light was just a short distance further. She could see there were gates and people moving about.

She picked up speed and her emotions skyrocketed with excitement. The light had filled the sky with splendor, much more beautiful than she had imagined.

It was so much more glorious up close than it had been from a distance. Her feelings caused her heart to race.

Her heart was bouncing with joy. Her body had begun to tire, but not enough for her to stop. There was a breeze blowing gently to refresh her and the sound of sweet and joyful music lifted her to new heights of ecstasy.

Her heart was beating out a cadence of excitement.

Her body tingled with joy. Her eyes danced with expectation. She was almost there! She could smell the sweet essence of flowers.

She swooned within at the odors so delightful. She could not believe her five senses. She was experiencing emotions and feelings as she never had before.

Suddenly she had arrived! She was approaching the gates with thanksgiving and to her great surprise, everyone present was waiting. There was no bickering, no sadness, no fighting, no pushing or shoving, and no strife.

11

12

Hosannas rang clear, echoing throughout the heavens and the whispers were those of excitement and acceptance.

The great gates were made of pearl, gleaming in the light. The streets were of pure, clear gold.

There was a fountain flowing from the throne, and the majesty of it all was breathtaking.

Throngs and throngs of people lined the way as she approached and there was such a feeling of excitement. She had not realized the importance of her arrival. The air vibrated with the joy and grandeur of her entrance.

There were angels with wings a flutter and their trumpets calling out her arrival. The trumpets resounded regally. As she entered this glorious place, there were no memories of pain. There were row upon row of family and friends who had gone before her, but her journey was so special.

Their faces mirrored the joy at her arrival and her beauty.

As she stepped through the gates, her bruised and scraped hands, feet and knees were no longer bruised and scraped. Her skin looked like baby's skin. And instead of her hair being disheveled from the long journey, it was transformed into a beautiful arrangement of order and beauty.

Her tattered dress had become a beautiful gown with a train that trailed for yards and yards. Her humble walking shoes became gorgeous slippers.

Though her trip had seemed like minutes, it had taken years, for time has a way of changing once it is past. All the memories and heartaches of her journey had become a mere wisp which quickly fluttered out of sight or senses.

Now, breathlessly, she began to approach her love and a song rose from the depths of her heart.

It was a melody of deliverance and healing.

A song of praise and adoration for her love.

He awaited her with joy and much reverence.

This, His love, had gone through great struggles and trials to get here. She had passed every test and, with great success, she had been refined, molded, and conformed to the comely woman that took her place with her beloved. Her beauty was beyond compare and her heart was without blemish. She was forgiven! She was redeemed!

She had been wounded and battered for her undaunted courage and faith, and He knew all about her. He was ecstatic with compassion, hope, joy, and a sense of satisfaction. The time had come. She was here at last!

As she approached Him, their eyes met and their hearts leaped. All she had been through was no more. There was only now and eternity to see.

Her eyes sparkled with emotion and expectation.

She was to rule with her Husband and King from this day forward and their hearts were entwined.

She had known that her goal would be wonderful.

This truly surpassed all words and expression and could only be expressed through praises. You see, this is the redeemed bride of Christ. He laid His life down for her to give her life and life more abundantly.

The two touched hands and turned to greet the heavenly throng overflowing the streets and on the clouds applauding. They cried out and sang exuberantly, "Hosanna to the King," "Glory, Glory, Glory," "Holy is the Lamb of God."

To look at the two of them, it would seem as if they had never seen pain or heartache. She had a glow that only reflected His love. As she gazed into His eyes, she saw her own beauty bathing in that tremendous love. At last, I am my beloved's and He is mine!

Her heart beat so loudly within her bosom, it seemed all of Heaven could hear. Her beloved, in royal array, stood grandly at her side. He looked at her as if He heard the beat of her heart when it was actually His heart beating as well. Now the two hearts beat as one. They would move, and breathe as one. She lives and breathes and has her being in Him.

The Bride Has Come!

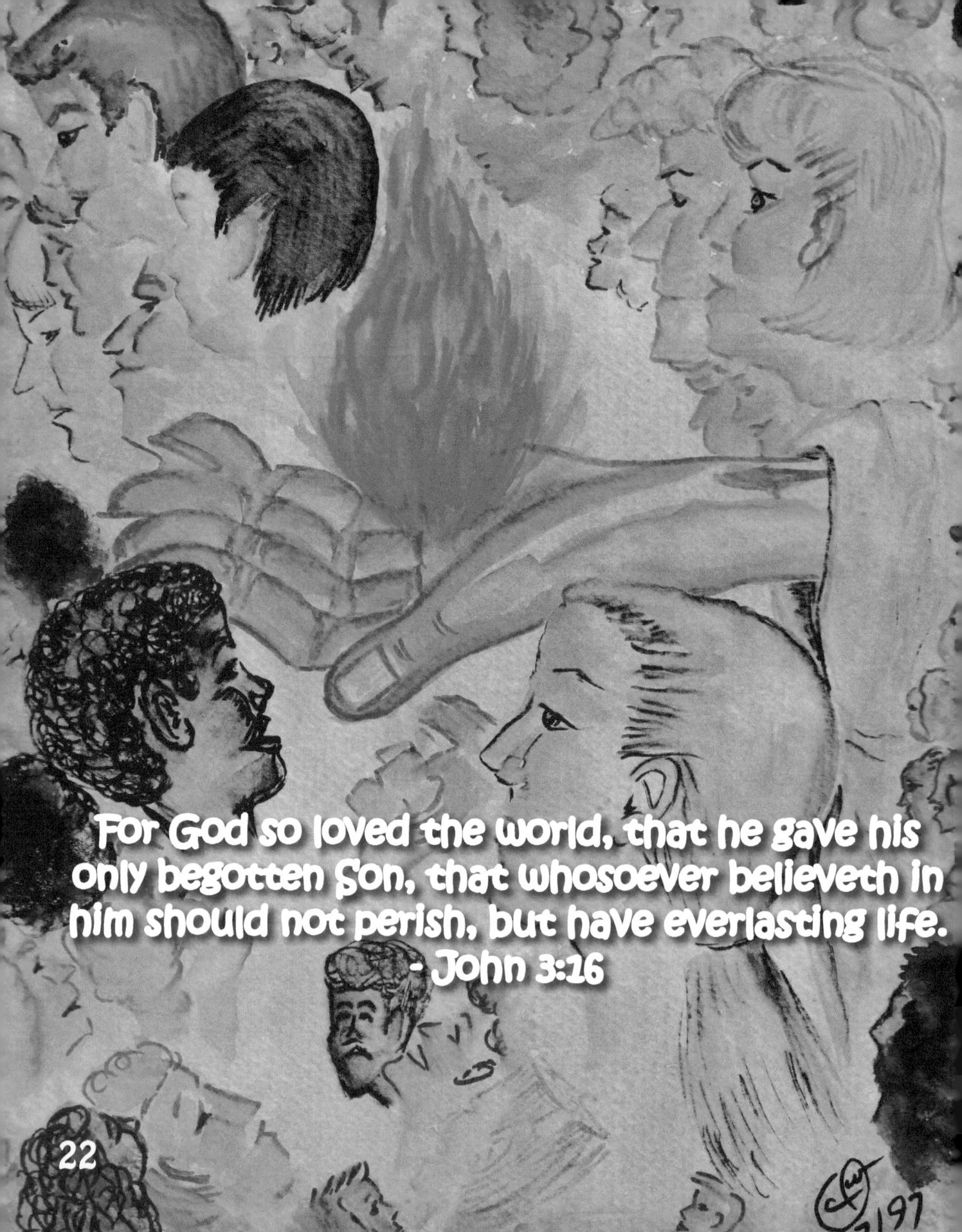

For God so loved the world, that he gave his only begotten Son, that whosoever believeth in him should not perish, but have everlasting life.
- John 3:16

22

In her recent book "Poking Holes in the Darkness" Christian writer Collene Martin shares personal devotions and short stories filled with Faith, Hope, Love and Purpose.

This book is currently available from the Author and through AMAZON.com

www.ingramcontent.com/pod-product-compliance
Lightning Source LLC
Chambersburg PA
CBHW041005170626
46815CB00002B/171